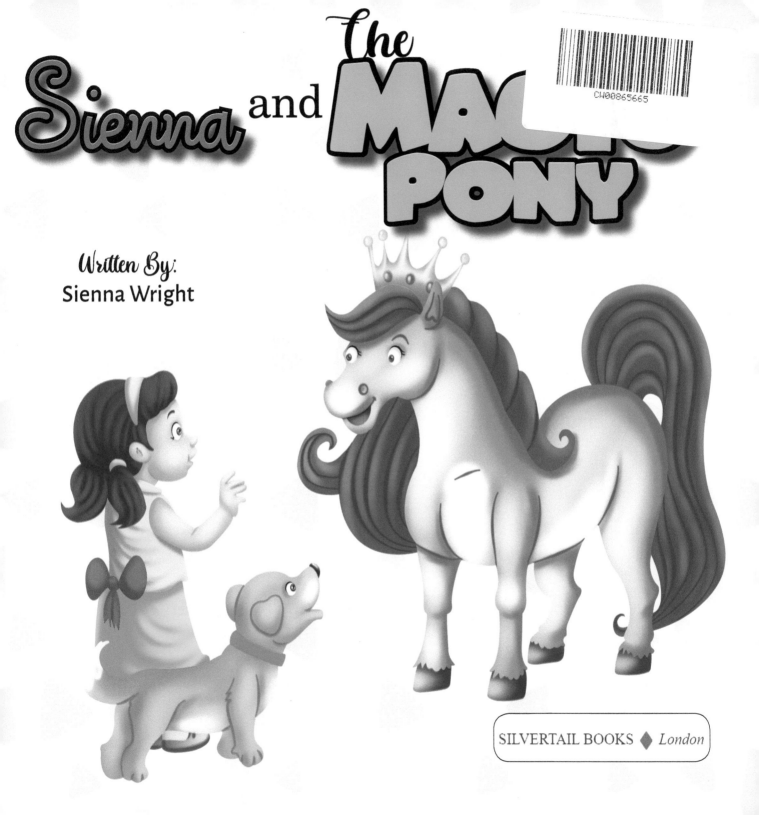

Sienna and The MAGIC PONY

Written By:
Sienna Wright

SILVERTAIL BOOKS ♦ London

First published in Great Britain by Silvertail Books in 2021

www.silvertailbooks.com

Illustrated and Designed by Attraente Design "www.attraentedesign.com"

A catalogue record of this book is available from the British Library

978-1-913727-15-4

Dedication

I dedicate this book to my teachers
Mr Warren and Mrs Huntley
for inspiring me to write this book

Once upon a time there was a land full of Magic Ponies.

There was a special way into the place where the Magic Ponies lived. It went through a waterfall where a special gateway opened next to an ancient willow tree.

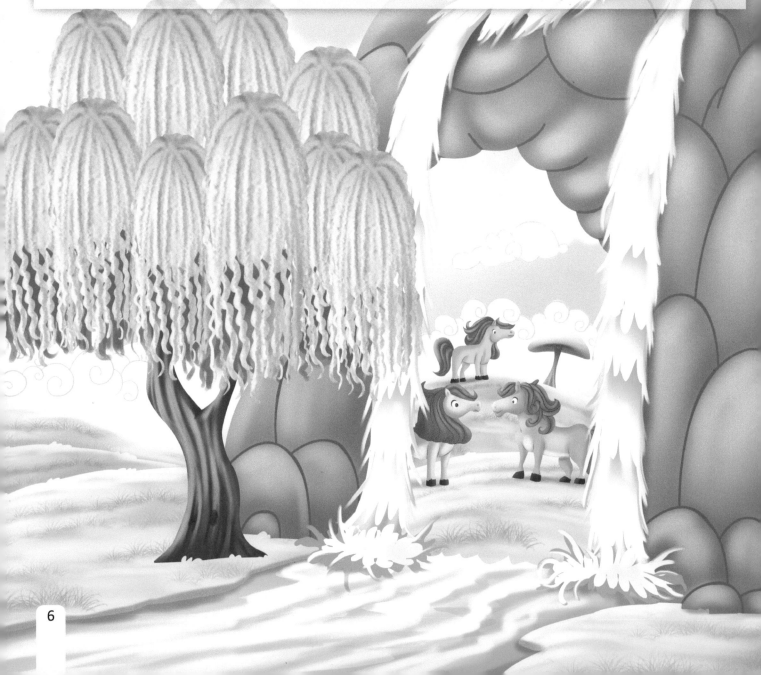

One day Sienna was walking her dog Teddy when she stopped to have a bite of her sandwich under the ancient willow tree.

The magic waterfall opened in front of her. Sienna turned and said, "WOW! Teddy, look at all the Magic Ponies in the special land behind the waterfall!"

She walked over to the waterfall and made her way into the field full of Magic ponies.

One of the Magic Ponies came over to see her. She said she was the Princess Pony and her name was Roseanna.

She invited Sienna and Teddy to join her on an adventure to the top of the Ponies' Magic Mountain.

Sienna got on the back of Roseanna and she galloped with Teddy running beside her.

On the way up to the Magic Mountain, Roseanna let Sienna stop and try some of their special berries which were called doodle berries. They were red and tasted like strawberries and blueberries mixed together. They were delicious.

As they reached the top of the Magic Mountain Roseanna told Sienna, "Now we are at the top of the Magic Mountain everything you touch will turn into the things you most wish to play with."

So Sienna touched a small tree which turned into a bike and she touched a flower which turned into a fluffy pink teddy bear.

Sienna was amazed. She was so happy she gave Roseanna a big cuddle.

The sun was setting on the Magic Mountain. It was almost time to go home so Sienna, Teddy and Roseanna galloped down towards the magic waterfall.

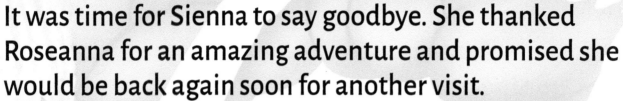

It was time for Sienna to say goodbye. She thanked Roseanna for an amazing adventure and promised she would be back again soon for another visit.

The End

Colour the Picture

Colour the Picture